ROGER PRICE'S

THE

TOMORROW PEOPLE

THE FIRST ONE

GARY RUSSELL

The Tomorrow People: The First One
Written by Gary Russell
Published in 2024 by
Oak Tree Books
oaktreebooks.uk

in association with
Chinbeard Books

Editor: Paul Simpson
Commissioning/Sub-Editor: Barnaby Eaton-Jones

Cover artwork: Robert Hammond
Layout and Typesetting: Joe Larkins

Gary Russell

The Tomorrow People

in

THE FIRST ONE

A Chinbeard Books / Oak Tree Books Original

Contents

Acknowledgements. vi

About The Tomorrow People vii

Cold Opening 1

Episode One 6

Episode Two 43

Episode Three. 81

For PVC…

*with love, respect and thanks for proving you can
meet your heroes and discover they are exactly
as you always hoped they would be.
You'll be missed forever.*

The author would like to thank:

Jason Haigh-Ellery and Nigel Fairs for letting me play in the sandpit nearly twenty-five years ago and Barnaby Eaton-Jones for the offer to play again. Andy Davidson for generosity and sharing continuity, laughs and gossip. Paul Simpson for being the bestest and most sympathetic copy-editor on the planet (watch him try to take the word "bestest" out now…) And most of all to Roger Price for giving us these amazing characters and worlds in the first place.

The Tomorrow People

If you've never met the Tomorrow People before… their names are John Dixon, Stephen Jameson, Carol MacNeil and Kenny Green. They seem to be just ordinary kids. A bit quieter than most, perhaps. They are not from a distant future, they live on Earth, here and now. They are The Tomorrow People, forerunners of a new race, *homo superior* or even *homo novus*, which is why they are reasonably young. They are nature's response to man's aggression: a new species, wiser and more peace-loving than *homo sapiens*, for they cannot kill. They have gained remarkable powers: they can talk to each other by thought waves – telepathy. They can influence objects in the same way – telekinesis or psychokinesis. And they can think themselves from place to place as well – teleportation, but they call it jaunting. They wear a jaunting belt to help them with the complex details of navigation (and to ensure they don't end up underwater, or inside a brick wall) but they don't need it for short jaunts when they know where they are going and can picture it in their minds.

Until more of their race evolve, or "break out" as they call it, these four have intergalactic responsibility for the future of planet Earth, under the guidance of the Galactic Federation, based aboard their impossibly huge space-station, known colloquially as the Trig. The Galactic Federation have gifted the Tomorrow People a biotronic living computer known as TIM (Technobiologically Informed Mentor), to help and guide them. TIM has been installed in a secret laboratory where, when they are not in their normal homes, the Tomorrow People can meet, work, play and even sleep and eat. The Lab itself was built by John, underneath an old disused London Underground station, where no one ever goes.

The Tomorrow People also have friends that aren't part of their new evolution, two very ordinary humans called Ginge and Lefty who were originally part of a plan to harm them. However, the duo saw the error of their ways and turned on their evil master, Jediakah, and so now help the Tomorrow People in whatever purely human way they can.

With thanks to Roger Price and Brian Finch.

THE FIRST ONE

Cold Opening

"Anderson Lewis House is a large place, what was once referred to as a 'country estate'. About twelve bedrooms, a few withdrawing rooms, massive kitchens in the basement and a series of halls and reading rooms on the ground floor. It had been in the McAllister family for centuries, its last owner being Oliver McAllister. Or 'Loony Liver' as the locals called him, for reasons we don't know.

"The National Trust had offered to buy it back in 1968, under their Land Scheme, but the owners, the Conner-Allens of Gloucestershire, despite not living down in Anderson Lewis House itself, were unwilling to part with it. Then last year, in early January 1972, the family finally moved in, having sold their Gloucestershire home in Podsmore Vale. And that is where, apparently, it all started to go wrong…"

John sat back on the soft bench close to TIM and sighed. "And that's about as much as I know. Anything else TIM?"

"Thank you, John," TIM purred. "I believe you have summed up the situation quite adequately."

"Oh please, don't flatter me," John muttered, raising his eyes as TIM's use of the word 'adequately'.

Carol stifled a grin at John's outrage, but Stephen wasn't so tactful.

"Awww, TIM, you've hurt John's feelings," Stephen said, his impish eyes glinting with mischief. "I mean, he probably had to go to the library and read a book or something to get all that."

John half-heartedly chucked an apple across the Lab at Stephen, but the younger boy just caught it, smiled, and took a huge bite out of it.

"Okay TIM, what can you tell us that I missed?" John stared directly up at the tubes and lights of their biotronic computer, as if a hard stare would make TIM feel guilty.

TIM of course 'felt' nothing. Instead, it offered another observation. "I am aware that Mister Harding and Mister Leftridge are outside the Lab, requesting admittance."

"Oh please let them in, TIM," said Carol and in response, the massive door to their secret Lab slid open and in strode Ginge and Lefty.

Both were in their usual biker gear, although as always, they had parked their bikes some way away from the old, unused Mark Lane tube station's entrance, to ensure no one could trace where they were going. With Jedikiah long gone, John was pretty confident that they were unlikely to be attacked in the Lab, but he still asked Ginge and Lefty to take precautions. It never hurt to be prepared, John always said.

And often, when he did say it, Stephen and Kenny would cheekily do a cub scout three-fingered salute behind his back. They never knew if he'd seen them, but Carol certainly had, and she'd given them both a warning sigh and shake of her head.

Kenny was Ginge's first subject in fact as he and Lefty settled down in a couple of chairs TIM somehow made pop out of thin air. "Where's the kid?" asked Ginge. Kenny had been instrumental in brokering a peace between Ginge and Lefty and the Tomorrow People when they first met, and the two bikers always felt protective towards him because of that.

Carol beamed proudly. "Kenny's been sent away," she said. "He's the first of us that the Galactic Federation have used to represent Earth on another planet. He's on Spyra. Apparently, this is the first step in the Federation fully admitting Earth into their union."

"The kid? An ambassador? Wow."

"Yeah, we can't believe it either," murmured Stephen, but again there was a twinkle in his eye because, like the others, Stephen was really missing Kenny's sardonic wit and hard-done-by self-deprecation – plus the two boys were similar ages, whereas both John and Carol were a few years older which, to Stephen made them seem positively ancient. And bossy. And… ugh, parental.

So yeah, he missed Kenny. Stephen had loads of mates; Anthony, Malcolm, Seth, Toaster (no one could pronounce his actual name), Sanjeev and Rebecca, but Kenny was the only one he could really be himself with because the others didn't know about him being a Tomorrow Person. He could hardly walk into Claremont Heath Secondary Modern and start jaunting everywhere or reading Rebecca's mind or making the vaulting horse in the sports hall move itself. Stephen had particularly enjoyed teasing Kenny that, with a school year between them,

Stephen had recently become old enough to ditch his school uniform and wear whatever he liked to school. Kenny had retorted that he didn't care because at his school, no one cared about uniforms anyway.

And now there he was, billions of light-years away, probably forced to wear one of those awful Galactic Trig robes and a silly hat. Stephen smiled, imagining Kenny's discomfort at that and probably wishing he was wearing his school blazer and trousers now.

John's cough brought Stephen out of his reverie and back into the present.

"Anyway, Lefty, tell us again why you think what's going on at Anderson Lewis House meant that I had to do all that research?"

Lefty looked at Ginge – Lefty rarely said very much, and when he did it rarely lasted more than twenty seconds and was usually "Yes, Ginge" or "No, Ginge" or "I really wanted a Harley". Now here he was with an audience, and he couldn't have looked more uncomfortable and awkward if he tried.

"G'wan," Ginge said, presumably wanting to sound encouraging but actually barking at Lefty, like he was giving an order.

"Well," Lefty stammered. "It all began with my Auntie June…"

Episode One

It had actually begun a few weeks before Lefty's Auntie June got involved.

Benjamin Conner-Allen and his wife Pauline had felt quite relieved knowing that Christmas 1971 would be their last in Podsmore Vale. They had a nice cottage set in a certain amount of land that most of the neighbours were probably jealous of, but the place had belonged to Pauline's mother and when they had inherited it, it already needed a lot of work done to it. Benjamin was not one of nature's natural handymen and although some money had been spent on various local builders, most of them aborted the jobs they were paid to do, leading to a lot of speculation down the Golden Harp that Mrs Conner-Allen was not the easiest of people to work for. One day she wanted the cottage walls painted. Then it was wallpaper. Then plain wallpaper that might get painted later.

Then when that was all done, no, she wanted the latest floral wallpaper after all. Then there were the ceilings, the electrics, the carpets… Pauline Conner-Allen clearly wasn't someone whose mind did not remain "absolutely and unequivocally made up" for more than ten minutes at a time.

Therefore, the cottage had remained in a constant state of half-done repairs and decoration for a good fifteen years, during which time two children had swelled the family. The eldest of these was Joseph, who frequently upset his parents because, by the time he approached teenager status, announced he no longer wished to be called Joseph at home, but the "absolutely common" name Joe, as that was what "my real mates call me". Benjamin had foolishly tried to inform his son that Joe was a name reserved for plumbers and ticket sellers at Gloucester railway station, but sulky Joseph rebelled by refusing to acknowledge any name other than Joe.

The complete opposite to him was the younger child, their daughter Samantha (oh no, never Sam), who was as angelic and sweet as her parents had hoped. The tittle-tattle in the Golden Harp tended to be that Joe was probably okay, but Samantha was quite likely to grow into what the locals referred to as a "proper little madam".

It was not seen as anything other than an excuse for a party in the pub when Benjamin let it be known that the family were selling the cottage and moving to some old pile they had inherited years ago, down on the edges of London, with more bedrooms and living rooms than any family of four could ever need.

At the party, actually held three weeks after the Conner-Allens had departed (just to make sure they didn't change their minds and come back), a toast was raised by Gloucester's finest builders, plumbers and electricians in honour of their equivalents in the region of Anderson Lewis house (wherever that was) who were going to need to seek early retirement as soon as the Conner-Allens arrived.

As it turned out, the tradesmen of Hertfordshire could relax, as the Conner-Allens found the minor Georgian splendour of Anderson Lewis House charming. The place had been renovated inside quite recently when trying to attract the National Trust's interest by Benjamin's eccentric uncle Oliver, but he had passed away before the deal was done, leaving the property to Benjamin.

Joe and Samantha were less inclined to love the place. It was quite a long way from the new schools they had both been forced to go to, requiring, in

Joe's case, a lengthy walk to a bus stop and then two buses to school. Samantha of course was driven to school by her mother as her Primary was closer than Joe's Grammar.

Both children found the huge place inhospitable and a bit, if they were honest, scary. Floorboards squeaked, curtains blew and shadows followed them. Truth was, two thirds of the house was unused by the Conner-Allens, but when Pauline had mooted the idea of selling it to a hotel chain, Benjamin had been appalled. The children, of course, had supported this idea and after one term at their new schools had decided moving somewhere else, preferably back to where they had come from, was ideal. Joe, in particular, received significant teasing for his Gloucester accent, another reason to resent his parental units, and had at least once tried getting on a train "home" to go and see his "mates" from his old school, until intercepted by Benjamin demanding to know where he'd got the money from.

To this day, no-one but Joe knew the answer to that.

Eighteen months passed. Joe settled into his teenager sulks more frequently now whilst Samantha was beginning to enjoy the house and its gardens more. One worried friend of Pauline's had commented to another that Samantha had the look of a child who had not only decided what changes she was going to make to the place once her parents had passed away, but quite possibly was already working out how to make that day come sooner than later.

One of the treats the children had been given when they first moved into Anderson Lewis House was a brand-new colour television in their playroom up on the first floor. Both Joe and Samantha made a lot of use of this and the playroom they'd been given. After all, there wasn't much else to. However, both resented the name 'playroom', as it was something they'd also had in Podsmore Vale but when they were five. The playroom was quite a large spare bedroom, and as well as the television, also contained lots of books, Samantha's toys (Joe was too old for toys, he had decided, before leaving Gloucester) and a record player.

Under the window was a large column-style radiator. It was covered in dirt and dust and, according to Joe, probably no one had cleaned behind it in a thousand years.

But in winter it happily gave out a good deal of heat, so both children were quite content.

They had been watching television together one April Sunday evening – well Samantha was, Joe was in the room and not really taking much notice of whatever was on. It was either that thing set at Follyfoot Farm or that other thing about a horse called Black Beauty. Samantha was at the age where horses were important and aspirational. Her parents dreaded the inevitable "Daddy, buy me a pony" that was bound to come from her watching such things. Joe secretly couldn't wait to see their response. If they said no, Samantha would make their lives unbearable. If they said yes, Joe already had a lengthy list of what *he* required to make things fair.

What happened that early evening seemed more weird than anything else.

As they both stared at the television, they were both distracted by a noise.

A mouse?

Then from behind the column radiator, well through one of the gaps really, rolled a biscuit. A perfectly round biscuit. Thick and chunky, probably some wholemeal thing.

It rolled out from behind the radiator and across the room. Both of them stared in surprise as it rolled, wobbled and finally fell.

After a few seconds, Joe gingerly reached out, then whipped his hand back. It was slightly soggy and very dirty, with a bit of cobweb on it.

Samantha instinctively whimpered a bit.

"Where did that come from?" Joe said. Then he turned to his sister. "You hiding biscuits from Mum?"

But Samantha shook her head, and her face had a look on it that told Joe she wasn't lying. And he certainly hadn't placed it there.

After a few moments, he scooped it up, crossed to the window, opened it and chucked it out for the birds.

Samantha frowned. "It looked like it had been there for years."

"Centuries maybe," Joe said, enjoying the moment. "Perhaps someone left it there. A ghost."

Samantha wasn't quite so old that the idea of a ghost didn't alarm her. After all there were those creaking floorboards, billowing curtains and long shadows in the rest of the house.

"The ghost biscuit," Joe continued. "Wooooohh!"

Samantha gave her big brother a good hard slap on his leg and went back to watching the horses.

But both she and Joe kept a wary eye on the radiator for the rest of the evening.

After a couple of days they had forgotten all about it, and never mentioned it to their parents. Which was unfortunate because a tip-off might have made them happier later.

*

The next weird thing that happened was witnessed by Benjamin and Pauline. It was an early summer's evening, still quite light outside, and very dry and warm.

The couple were standing opposite one another in the kitchen, next to the sink, drinking tea and discussing Benjamin's work.

Pauline suddenly stopped talking. She was looking down at their feet. Benjamin looked at her, then followed her gaze.

There were their own feet on the kitchen floor. Pauline wearing a nice pair of low-heeled slipons. Benjamin in moccasins. But, in a neat circle around their feet, were a series of muddy footprints. Wet muddy footprints. And there were two very exceptional things about this, putting aside that on a warm summer night, no footprints should be wet.

Firstly, the footprints were in a tight circle around their own feet. Which would have been impossible to make because it would mean whoever made them would have to have pretty much walked through the sink and cupboards to do so.

Secondly, the wet prints didn't match either pair of shoes that the Conner-Allens were wearing.

These were wet, muddy boot prints, chunky and heavy, but quite small. Like a child's boot print.

Certainly too small for Joe, who was upstairs.

And Samantha didn't own a pair of boots like this, plus she was out at a local Girl Guides meeting – in fact, Benjamin was due to drive out to collect her very soon.

Neither of them said anything, but they both looked at each other, frowning. Finally, Pauline said a sort of half-gasped "How the heck…"

Benjamin bent down and wiped his finger through the boot prints. Wet mud indeed. Now on his fingertip.

He looked at it as if he'd never seen mud before. As though some alien ooze were suddenly on his finger.

He wiped it off on a tea towel, eliciting a slight noise of frustration from his wife.

"Must be the kids…" was his only comment, but he knew that wasn't true. Those prints simply hadn't been there five minutes ago. Two minutes ago.

Pauline wasn't quite so sanguine about it at all. "Where did they come from?"

"Are you sure Mrs Kingdom didn't bring one of her children today when she came cleaning?"

Pauline shook her head. "Mrs Kingdom's not due till tomorrow and she never brings Alexander. Not after that time he brought the dog and—"

Benjamin knew that story well enough, so he cut his wife off. "Look, I'm sure there's a perfectly reasonable explanation. And while I drive over to get Samantha, I'll try and work out what it is." He smiled at Pauline, scooped up the Granada's keys and was out the back door as quickly as possible.

He'd barely reached the car when he heard Pauline scream.

It was an odd noise, he thought, and reflected later that he had never heard his wife actually scream before. On the whole, most people could say they go through life never actually needing a reason to let out a noise as loud and soul-gutting as that. Something so primal and tortured.

So, upon hearing it, Benjamin had no hesitation in walking, or running, back inside his home.

Pauline was shaking and pointing at the hallway.

After checking she wasn't actually injured, Benjamin followed the direction of her point.

Out in the hallway were a series of booted child's wet footprints that most assuredly hadn't been there moments earlier.

Benjamin Conner-Allen then realised why his wife's scream had been so particularly blood-curdling. As he watched, more footprints came into existence, as if some invisible person with small but heavy feet was stamping randomly around the house's hallway, leaving a brand-new series of muddy marks. Round and round and round and—

They stopped.

Just like that. Benjamin had never really understood the phrase "you could cut the atmosphere with a knife" until that exact moment, but the change was unearthly and bizarre. As soon as the footprints stopped being made, the whole house seemed to relax. If it was alive he'd believe it had sighed.

He looked back at Pauline, who was being sick in the kitchen sink.

He looked into the hallway again and gingerly walked to the phone, making sure he didn't step on any of the footprints in case that would start them up again. He called Mrs Kingdom, asked if she would mind awfully picking Samantha up from

Guides and keeping her at her house until he could get over soon, only his wife was feeling unwell and he couldn't leave her just yet.

He put the phone down and stared at the floor again.

No footprints. He looked everywhere. The floor was spotless.

He hurried back into the kitchen, where Pauline had plonked herself down in a chair. She looked at him as he gave her a cuddle, and he felt her tense. He guessed she'd looked over his shoulder and seen the clean floor.

Both of them looked back towards the sink.

No footprints.

None.

As if they had never been there.

"But we both saw them…" Benjamin muttered, saying what Pauline was probably thinking too.

"Did you call?" asked a voice behind them.

It was Joe, stereo headphones round his neck, holding the cable he'd unplugged before coming downstairs. "I wasn't sure, sorry. You okay?"

"Your mother's not feeling well," Benjamin said. "Go back up and listen to your Bolans and Bowies or whatever, we'll be up shortly."

Presumably impressed by his father's sudden

accurate awareness of his musical tastes, Joe did as he was told.

Benjamin cleaned up the sink. "Do we tell the kids?" he finally asked.

"Tell them what?" Pauline asked. "If we can't explain it to each other, what would we say to them?"

*

The third and final straw was a few weeks later.

The whole family were gathered in the huge lounge room, watching television. It was only the news, BBC version of course. It was one thing to let Samantha and Joe watch series for children on ITV, but grown-up television was always the BBC.

Although the news was on, no one was really taking much notice; they were actually talking for once. Samantha was asking Pauline about some Girl Guide weekend away in the New Forest and Benjamin was talking to Joe about getting his hair cut.

Samantha and Pauline were on the sofa. Benjamin was in an armchair next to that, but Joe was to the side of the TV so he couldn't really see it straight on. Beyond his chair was a recessed alcove of bookshelves and Joe was slightly leaning against them.

Benjamin was about to tell his son for the umpteenth time not to do precisely that, when Joe let out a yelp.

Benjamin hadn't really seen what had happened, but his wife and daughter certainly did.

Joe for his part was rubbing his right shoulder, then stopped and bent down, picking something up.

"What hit you?" Samantha asked her brother.

"'Hit you'?" repeated Benjamin. "What do you mean, something hit him?"

But Joe was holding up a coin. "This," he muttered. "Oh, and ouch. That hurt, in case anyone's interested."

Samantha crossed over and took it from his fingers. She rolled it round, looking at it carefully. "George Rules," she read the inscription. She turned it over. "North Wales."

Benjamin retrieved it. "It's an old coin, eighteenth century going by the King George head on it. Where on Earth did you find this, Joe?"

"I didn't find it…" Joe started, but Pauline finally spoke from back on the sofa.

"It hit him," she said, slightly louder than she probably intended. "It just appeared in mid-air and smacked into him, like someone threw it. I saw it, Ben, I saw it!"

Benjamin frowned. "Darling, coins don't just appear in mid-air do they?" And then he stopped. He and his wife's eyes met, because they thought about bootprints appearing and disappearing.

"Ghost biscuit," Samantha said to Joe.

"What?" Both parents were looking at their children.

Over the next few minutes, the whole family detailed the incidents with the ghost biscuit from behind the radiator and ghost boot prints in the hall, and now a ghost ha'penny thrown at Joe's back.

Eventually Benjamin sat back in his chair. "There's no such things as ghosts."

"Then how do you explain all this?" his son argued.

Pauline answered slowly. "Well, there must be some strange magnetic force under the house and…"

The rest of the family just stared at her. "Well, all right," she snapped. "It's a ghost. This house is haunted."

Samantha crawled back onto the sofa next to her mother and hugged her for comfort.

Benjamin sighed. Joe grinned. "Yes, wait till I tell everyone at school about this. I can charge 10p per entry. 'Roll up, roll up, see the penny-throwing, biscuit-loving, muddy-footed ghost from the 1700s.'"

"Why are they from the 1700s?" Pauline asked.

"The coin," Joe smiled. "And anyway, didn't you say that's how old this house is? Probably some workman crushed when the roof collapsed while they were building it. Or a maid, drowned in the basement when the water pipes burst. Or..."

"Stop it," shrieked Samantha. "Stop it, stop it, stop it!"

Joe stopped.

For a few moments the family sat in silence while on the telly Robert Dougall talked about the Common Market or Vietnam.

Then Joe clicked his fingers as if remembering something else. He stood up and wandered over to a table and scooped up the paper. Not his father's *Daily Telegraph* but the local gazette. He flipped through some pages and then stabbed down at something he'd seen. "Here's what we need, Dad. And she's not that far away."

*

"And that's when Auntie June got involved," said Lefty.

He looked at everyone gathered around the up-lit central Link Table in the Lab, as if that explained everything.

"I'm not sure I follow you," Carol finally voiced what they were all thinking.

Lefty looked alarmed. He'd just spoken for even longer than any time in his life and now they wanted him to talk more.

"She's a medium," he finally said.

Stephen snorted. "They think they've got a real ghost?"

TIM's lights flared slightly lighter as they always did when he prepared to speak. "It is a reasonable assumption," he said.

Stephen snorted even louder. "Oh come off it, TIM. You can't tell me you believe in ghosts?"

"Stephen," pronounced TIM. "There are many things that can be explained by science and technology but there are also a lot of things we cannot always understand, no matter how advanced we are.'

"You'll be telling me you believe in magic and reading sheep's entrails next."

"As Arthur C Clarke said a few years ago, Stephen, to some people any sufficiently advanced technology is indistinguishable from magic."

John joined in. "Yes but TIM, we're talking ghosts here. Dead spirits come back to haunt an old house. I don't think so."

Carol however was on TIM's side.

"I think we should keep an open mind. After all, we can't say ghosts don't exist. We can rationalise them to some extent but surely even as Tomorrow People, we can't be so arrogant that we are sure of everything."

"Thank you, Carol," TIM said.

"Anyway," Lefty said again. "That's why Auntie June wanted me to tell you lot. She thought you could use your... head-talky stuff to help her during her seance, see if you can contact anyone."

"Head-talky stuff?" This was too much for Stephen who had to lie down on one of the Lab beds to giggle. "Head-talky stuff, I love it..."

John however took a different tack. "Hang on a moment, Lefty. How does your Auntie June know about our 'head-talky stuff' anyway?"

Lefty looked like a rabbit caught in headlights. "I told her."

Ginge thwacked his compatriot round the back of his head. "You idiot, Lefty," he said. "We promised to keep these kids' secret, well... secret."

"But you told your brother first…"

Ginge probably didn't need to see John's face to imagine the look he was getting.

"Ginge?" John prompted quietly, albeit with an edge of steel.

Ginge coughed. "Well one night Chris and I got a bit…"

"Drunk?" offered a grinning Stephen.

"Not sure you should know about the evil effects of alcohol, kid," Ginge said.

"I'm fourteen," Stephen said. "Not four. And don't try and change the topic of conversation."

"So, Lefty's Auntie knows about us," John said. "And Ginge's brother, Chris. Anyone else? I mean, should we be doing a cover feature for *Look and Learn*?"

"I am sure Ginge and Lefty's families are quite trustworthy," TIM interrupted. "Now, John, I think you should go and—"

"Ummm," Lefty coughed. "Auntie June made a request."

If John could have gritted his teeth any further, they'd be stumps as he spoke. "Yes?"

"Well, she said it would be better with… you know…." Lefty was waving towards Carol.

"Carol." Carol filled in the gap in Lefty's knowledge. "I mean it's only been eight months since we first met."

"Sorry," Lefty said. "Never very good with names. I mean, I still call Ginge 'Norman' half the time."

"Why would you do that?" asked John.

"It's his real name."

The only thing stopping Ginge from killing Lefty on the spot was the distraction of Stephen's hysterical laughter. "Norman. His name's Norman." Stephen was literally gasping for breath. "Nooooorman…"

And he was still giggling about hours later, long after Ginge, Lefty and Carol had left the lab. "His name's… Norman…."

*

Three Days Later…

Madam Juniper Rose, Medium to the Stars was, Carol decided, something else. Firstly, she had arrived at Anderson Lewis House on a motorbike. Carol, who of course had jaunted in to do a recon an hour earlier and was currently standing out of everyone's eyesight behind a big oak tree, knew very little about motor bikes, but she was pretty sure this was a bigger, faster, and heavier machine than either Ginge or Lefty had. She noted it said Triumph Daytona on the side, and there certainly seemed to be some modifications. The exhaust pipe was massive, and there were huge wicker panniers attached to the back that made the whole bike almost as wide as the Ford Granada also parked in the drive that Carol guessed belonged to Mr Conner-Allen.

Juniper Rose herself was wearing an old 1920s style helmet and had massive goggles over her eyes. She was wearing a long woven green coat, a bizarre orange woollen scarf that Carol had been convinced was going to get wrapped around the wheels if she wasn't careful, and a pair of cherry red Doc Marten boots that went up very high under the coat.

As Aunt Juniper dismounted, she dropped the goggles to her throat, revealing she was wearing a pair of blue-tinted Lennon-style sunglasses and more lipstick than any lady of an uncertain age really ought to be wearing.

She whipped off the helmet, revealing a shock of white hair that popped up into an almost beehive shape as the air reached it.

She undid the coat and gave herself a little shake, before turning to her panniers. She was portly without being overweight, and with the coat open,

Carol could see she was wearing a knee-length, one-piece, tie-dye linen dress that wouldn't have been out of place in Woodstock. And was that a hip flask on the belt?

Juniper Rose shoved her hand into the panniers and retrieved a smaller carpet bag, giving it a bit of a shake too.

Then she straightened up.

"You don't have to hide, my dear Miss MacNeil."

Carol stepped away from the tree, gingerly, hoping no one inside the house spotted her or they'd wonder why she hadn't arrived on the bike with Juniper Rose.

"It's all right, I told them you'd be here before me. I said you were coming up from Kings Cross on the chuff-chuff. But I assume you did your lovely teleportation thing, yes?"

Carol just nodded.

"Never fear, my dear. All your secrets are safe with me. Telepathy, telekinesis, teleportation, oh and I believe one of your little friends is a quite power psychometrist too."

Carol smiled. "Kenny. He's awfully good at it. He's away I'm afraid. A rather long way away in fact."

"Shame. I could have used him a few weeks ago at Major Lowe's place in Derby. He had a scrying stone that he thought came from Mars. Would have been interesting to know what your Kenny would have made of it. Would have added a bit of drama to a really rather dull afternoon after a tediously long journey to the Midlands."

"Was it really from Mars?"

"Oh dear sweet girl, no. It was a lump of glass from a gift shop in Ipswich. Silly old Major was on the receiving end of his wife's latest practical joke. Ha! His face. Oh dear, dear me yes."

"You seem to know a lot about…"

"Your special powers. ESP and all that? Course I do. Been studying it for years, waiting for people like you to start popping up regularly. Time for you to start changing the world, my dear."

"Well," Carol admitted. "That's the plan, certainly."

"Good, good. Meanwhile we have a Georgian house with a Georgian ghost. I assume Lefty told you everything we know so far."

Carol nodded. Then she remembered a promise she'd made, albeit reluctantly. "What's Lefty's real name?"

Juniper Rose grinned. "Lefty, of course."

"No I mean, his *real* name. We call him Lefty

because of his surname, but we just realised we don't know his real name."

"My dear, his name is Lefty. It's on his birth certificate. My darling sister and her daft brother were wonderful old dropouts after the war, conscientious objectors and all that. Calling him Lefty Leftridge was just another of their cocking-a-snoot at the establishment things. I love them for it."

Carol laughed. And then realised Juniper Rose was deadly serious. His name really was Lefty.

"Now, can you use your telepathy to talk to me?"

Carol shook her head. "I'm afraid it doesn't work that way. Only with other Tomorrow People."

"Thought so, never mind. We'll cope. While I'm doing all the theatrics with the candles and closed curtains and pretending to be in touch with the spirits, I need you to see if there really is someone else you can find a way to communicate with. Or whether it's this couple's children, as I suspect. When I came up here last week to meet them all, I found them… odd. The girl is ghastly, to be frank. But the teenage boy, well he's getting to that age where everything is seen as an attack on him. Finding his identity and all that, makes him number one suspect to me."

Carol nodded. A boy hitting puberty. It could mean he was breaking out, a potential new Tomorrow Person. "And the parents?" she asked.

"Hideous middle-class people with delusions of grandeur. He's idle rich, living off money earned by relatives years ago. She's a social climber, with a chip on her shoulder about her origins in a Manchester slum. If you ask me, people who grow up in Northern terraces are the salt of the Earth and will one day make this country great again. People who are ashamed of their class and backgrounds, well, I have no time for any of them."

Carol shrugged. "I try not to judge people," she said, perhaps a little more tartly than she meant.

Juniper Rose just laughed. "Oh please, my dear. I say as I find. Doesn't always make me right, but it certainly keeps people on their toes. Don't be offended."

"Our research," Carol said, changing the subject swiftly, "suggests that they've not been here very long."

"Less than a year," Juniper Rose confirmed. "Inherited it after old Loony Liver popped his clogs. The locals thought he went a bit insane near the end, after his wife passed away. He spent his last few months talking to himself, or inanimate objects;

convinced he was holding conversations with table lamps, or wirelesses, or coffee mugs. Wish I'd met him, he sounds like my kind of chap."

They began walking to the front door, ready to announce their presence.

"So, the medium stuff, it's all an act, is it?"

Juniper Rose winked at her. "I said drama, I didn't say an act. I have contacted lots of spirits over the years. But most of them aren't in situations like this. This is theatricality. But once in a blue moon, under it all, can be a real presence. So, if we can rule out the son, then on the surface, this one's a bit of a cheeky poltergeist, having fun at the Conner-Allens' expense. But that's not to say it couldn't turn nasty on a whim. The theatricality is more a front, a disguise to relax the homeowners. It's what they expect. But if something does show up, it's easier to make them think its part of the drama and avoid hysterics. Or a repeat of 1967."

"What happened in 1967?"

"Something I can't afford to have a repeat of," was all Juniper Rose said on that.

Carol didn't feel reassured.

Lefty's Auntie June was definitely not what she had expected at all.

John and Stephen were sat in the Lab around the under-lit Link Table, hands splayed on its surface, fingertips just touching, to boost their powers.

"Carol, how's it going?" John asked telepathically.

"Auntie June is a character," Carol replied in the same way. "But there's something about her that has me on edge?'

"Why? Is she dangerous?"

"Oh no, no, I don't think so. No, I think she's far more real than she, well, presents herself. I get the feeling she's seen things and hides it all underneath what she calls 'drama'."

"Hey, did you do what I asked?" Stephen butted in.

"I did. And I know the answer."

Stephen grinned. More ammunition for later. "And?"

"And I'm not telling you his real name. It's private."

"I imagine Lefty will be grateful for your discretion, Carol," said TIM.

Stephen pursed his lips in disappointment. "I'll find out eventually."

"We're inside the house now," Carol continued. "The Conner-Allens have sent the children away, which is a nuisance."

"Why?"

"Well TIM, something Auntie June said made me wonder if the boy, Joe, might be one of us. Breaking out."

"You think he's causing the manifestations?" asked John.

"Well, I think it's a possibility. So does Auntie June, although not so much from a Tomorrow Person point of view, but more a mischievous kid pranking his parents." Carol stopped abruptly.

"Carol?"

"Sorry. Auntie June is discussing her new hair or something with Mrs Conner-Allen, not sure what that's about, and her husband is asking me how I want my tea. Look John, Stephen. I'm going to stay quiet now, but we'll link up shortly when the séance starts. I want you two and TIM to hear everything that's going on during that."

"Okay," said John. "Speak shortly."

"I think we should go to Anderson Lewis House," Stephen said suddenly.

"Why?" asked TIM.

Stephen looked up at the computer. "Something in Carol's voice. I think she's more scared than she's letting on."

"Don't worry," John said. "If she needs us, we can be there in seconds."

*

Pauline Conner-Allen, Carol reckoned, was terrified. Benjamin however was utterly contemptuous about Juniper Rose.

A small reading room had been turned into the séance area. A circular table was positioned in its centre. The windows covered by long, heavy closed drapes. The table covered in a lace cloth that Juniper Rose had brought with her, along with a couple of ornate silver candlesticks that were popped at its centre. A few other candles were in various places in the room, and Carol had been instructed to go through the house and turn off anything electrical except the fridge.

This had been prearranged with Juniper Rose, giving Carol a chance to do some snooping – it was actually utterly irrelevant to the séance.

Carol had found the house relatively as she had expected, a modernised Georgian house, although many of the upstairs rooms were disused and hadn't been altered since the turn of this century. So the whole place was a mix of Georgian design, some Victorian updates and significant 1960s/1970s modernity.

"A perfect melting pot for poltergeist activity," Juniper Rose had whispered to her when Carol had remarked on this. "And no sign of Joseph or that frightful daughter?"

"I don't think there's anyone in this house other than us. Except…"

Juniper Rose was immediately alert. "Yes?"

"You remember that story about the muddy footprints?"

"Small child, hobnail boots, wet mud in early summer. Yes?"

Carol frowned. "Well, it's probably nothing…"

"Oh come along my dear, you are here to give me your impressions. You have skills and expertise even I lack, so out with it."

Carol sighed. "When I was in the kitchen, switching off the toaster, near the sink I thought I could see them. On the floor. More… peripherally. I mean when I looked at where I thought I saw them, nothing, no muddy prints at all. It was just a sideways look. As if I was seeing… somewhere else."

Juniper Rose was nodding. "I think I can rule out Joseph, the boy then. Seeing some sort of after image, a visual echo, is very common for special people. The rest of us can never see them."

Carol nodded. "It was only momentary."

As they made their way to the séance room, Juniper Rose stopped and grasped Carol's wrist. "Back when this house was built, when no one had heard words like telepathy and the rest of it, they had a name for people like you, who could go beyond the norm."

"Witches probably."

Juniper rose shook her head. "No, that was much earlier, although pretty much for the same reason. No, back when this house was built, they'd say people like you youngsters had second-sight. And you just demonstrated exactly why. You see things, as you said, on the periphery. Such a gift." Juniper Rose let Carol's wrist go with a tender pat. "I'm so very jealous, you know."

Then they had entered the room.

Thirty minutes later, candles lit, otherwise everything in darkness, Juniper Rose began the séance.

"Now this is not an exorcism," she assured the Conner-Allens. "That's not what I do. I contact, I discuss, I befriend. Usually that's enough to send them on their way and they leave you alone."

"They?" Benjamin Conner-Allen wasn't going to buy into this, Carol thought.

"Spirits. Ghosts. Poltergeists." Juniper Rose waved her hands melodramatically around her head, as if she was batting away cobwebs. Carol tried not to laugh. "My assistant here is, as I told you, here to record everything that happens in her big red book there."

Carol taped the huge red notebook Juniper Rose had given her earlier. Carol wasn't really going to write anything down, but it was the pretence with which she had been given admittance to Anderson Lewis House.

"However, if it is a dark spirit," Juniper Rose went on, "I can put you in touch with Reverend Cook who does that sort of thing. Quite cheaply, too." She held her hands out, palms up.

As instructed Carol took her right hand, Benjamin her left, while he took his wife's in his left and Pauline took Carol's.

They formed a circle, round a circular table, the darkness only punctuated by the flickering candles.

"Spirit!" Juniper Rose suddenly yelled, which made everyone jump, and tighten their grips on each other which was probably the intention. "Spirit, come to Madam Juniper Rose. I mean you no harm. No one in this house intends harm, we wish to converse, to discuss, to exchange words."

Carol admired the theatricality.

*

In the Lab, Stephen and John did too. Stephen was grinning as Carol had telepathically explained everything that Auntie June was saying, and what was going on.

"John," TIM broke in. "John, I am concerned."

Without breaking the link, knowing that Carol would hear them all, John asked why.

"I… I don't know. This feels wrong."

Stephen frowned. He'd never heard TIM 'concerned' before, in a way that suggested even TIM couldn't explain what the problem was. It made him sound even more human. Which was probably not a good thing right now.

"TIM, everything is fine," Carol assured him. "It's all a bit of pantomime. There's no one in this house other than the four of us in the room, I promise you."

"I hope you are correct, Carol," said TIM.

"Stay focussed everyone," said John, ever practical. He and Stephen closed their eyes, concentrating on keeping linked to Carol's mind.

"Stay with us, Carol," he murmured.

*

Back in the room at Anderson Lewis House, Carol was watching the other three. Juniper Rose had her eyes closed as she muttered incantations. Pauline had her eyes screwed up and closed in panic, trying not to make a sound. Benjamin had his eyes closed but his face had an expression that suggested this was the most idiotic thing he'd ever been asked to do.

While she was talking, calling the spirits, listing saints, Powers of This, Sacraments of That and the Hoary Hosts of the Other, Juniper Rose opened one eye to acknowledge Carol was doing her job, mentally scanning the room.

She actually gave Carol a wink and a grin before closing her eyes again.

Suddenly the candle nearest the door went out. The other three were unaware of this, but Carol jumped slightly.

Then another candle went out.

And another.

Juniper Rose was still chanting away.

Soon the only candle lit was the one at the centre of the table. Carol passed this information to her fellow Tomorrow People back at the Lab.

"It's actually a bit creepy and—"

Carol stopped speaking in her mind.

Facing her, stood beside Juniper Rose, was a scruffy lad of about 12 or 13, small, skinny, almost gaunt. He wore rough woollen clothing and a flat cap. Piercing blue eyes stared into hers. His face was dirty, from soot or something similar. Like he'd ben up a chimney.

The boy stepped forward, into the middle of the table, as if it wasn't really there. Or maybe *he* wasn't really there.

Perhaps Juniper Rose's words had got further into Carol's psyche than she had realised, because to all intents and purposes this was a ghost, passing through solid objects, staring straight into her face.

The boy smiled.

"Hullo, Carol," he said.

Except he didn't say it out loud. His lips hadn't moved.

He was a telepath!

"John, did you hear that?" Carol almost shouted out loud rather than telepathically.

"No, hear what?" said Stephen.

"They can't hear you, Carol," said the boy and he reached forward as if to take Carol's hands. Which was impossible of course because he was an insubstantial ghost standing in the middle of a solid table.

So why could Carol feel his small hands gripping hers.

"Help me, Carol. Help me please! This is a trap!"

*

In the Lab John suddenly yelled. "Carol? Carol??"

"We've lost her," Stephen gasped. "She's gone."

"TIM, get us to Anderson Lewis House now," commanded John, breaking the link and standing up, hands already gripping his jaunting belt.

Nothing happened.

"TIM?"

TIM's lights glowed and flared as he started to speak. But the voice that came from their biometric friend was not TIM's.

"You were given all the clues," said a powerful voice, mockingly. "You didn't take the hint to stay away. And now you are mine, Tomorrow People. Mine!"

And all hell broke loose in the Lab as an impossible wind literally blew Stephen and John off their feet and across the Lab, twisting and turning them in a massive psychic force that wouldn't let go, as all around them the replacement TIM voice howled with powerful laughter.

*

Back at Anderson Lewis House, Pauline Conner-Allen was screaming again.

Juniper Rose was sat dead still, bolt upright, eyes wide open, mouth apart as if in mid-sentence, but otherwise the woman was frozen, not moving, as if her brain had just been switched off.

Benjamin tried to revive her, waved a hand in front of her eyes. Nothing.

Then Pauline and Benjamin heard a noise, like a strange whispering.

Pauline had lost the ability to scream any more, she was beyond fear. All she and her husband could do was watch as the shadows seemed to move and twist and engulf Carol.

And when they faded, Carol's chair was empty.

It was as though she had never even been there.

Episode Two

"It was a demonstration of psychokinesis on a scale far grander and more powerful than anything a Tomorrow Person could currently achieve."

"Thanks, TIM," said Stephen. "That makes us feel so special."

"It is a statement of fact, Stephen. Powerful as you, John, Carol and Kenny are, none of you have the raw power capable of repeating what happened here in the Lab."

Stephen and John were bustling around the Lab, resetting everything that had been moved or broken during the attack. Stephen found one of the pillars that usually supported the Link Table lying on a chair. It was broken beyond repair. He rolled it towards the main entrance so it could be disposed of later.

The whole thing had ended as suddenly as it had started. Stephen and John were shaken but not actually hurt, a fact that TIM had also noted. "It was a warning, not an attack," TIM had surmised.

"What about Carol?" John demanded. "We need to jaunt to Anderson Lewis House right now."

"I'm sorry, John," said TIM. "That demonstration had a purpose, and that purpose was to stop you getting to help Carol right now."

"Why?"

"Because you noted that I was, to use Stephen's vernacular, 'taken over by a voice'. I have checked my internal chronometers and whilst for me, I was unaware of any of this, there is nearly a three-minute gap within my own logs that I cannot account for."

"Are you saying you *were* actually taken over?" Stephen frowned. "How?"

"I cannot answer that. I apologise. This has never happened before and I genuinely do not understand how it has, but my biological systems were indeed interrupted for one hundred and forty-seven seconds that I cannot account for. As a result, I cannot jaunt you anywhere until all my biotech-systems are fully rebooted and safe."

"How long, TIM?" snapped John.

"Within the next few moments. I will inform you when I can jaunt you both that distance safely and accurately."

"We could take the risk," Stephen said. "I mean, Carol might need us."

"I share your frustration," John said quietly. "But we're no use to Carol if, without TIM's control of our belts, we overshoot and end up in Holland or inside a concrete floor. We have to wait and hope Carol is okay."

Stephen rolled away another broken pillar, then threw a look at John. "Look, you've known TIM longer than any of us. You pretty much built him. How could someone take him over?"

John shrugged. "When the Federation installed him, I helped. But they did the really complicated bits, especially the stuff that designates him as 'alive'. We need to talk to the Sophostrian engineers that originally designed him to know that."

"I can hear you both," TIM said. "And whilst I understand your concerns, rest assured I am currently creating new protocols to hopefully block any further incursions into my systems."

"Hopefully?" Stephen repeated.

"More importantly, TIM," said John, "those protocols ought to have been in place already."

"I would suggest it is a sign of how powerful a force it was that it was able to do so. I would also point out that I was able to expel it relatively quickly."

"Sorry, TIM," said Stephen. "We didn't mean to sound rude."

But John was less conciliatory. "Actually no, TIM, that's not entirely acceptable. I want you to contact the Trig and let the relevant people know what happened. Not just for our benefit but for the benefit of other TIMs with guardianship over the equivalents of Tomorrow People on alien planets, and in the future too."

"Of course, John. Meanwhile, I am now sufficiently capable to jaunting you to the House."

John and Stephen crossed to the jaunting pad at the back of the Lab where TIM could focus his boosters and coordination. "Get us there now please, TIM."

And in a swirl of colour and sound, John and Stephen were on their way.

After a pause, TIM spoke to the empty Lab. "I know you heard all that."

"Of course I did," came the voice that had taken TIM over earlier. "Thank you for letting me do so. Next time, kindly don't fight me and there will be fewer… problems."

"I… understand," TIM replied. "I apologise."

And the laughter from the other voice began again.

*

She was still in Anderson Lewis House, Carol was sure of that. She had prowled the corridors earlier and the layout was the same. But it was much darker and less welcoming. The few curtains she could see were floral but thin and a breeze was blowing in through them.

A couple of rooms had fireplaces in them, and these were lit, although giving out light more than heat.

Or were they?

That was odd, Carol thought. She could see the moving curtains. She could see the flickering flames, and even some candles. What she couldn't do, she realised with surprise, was feel any warmth. Or the cold from the breeze coming in from the gardens. It was as if… as if she wasn't quite there.

She walked into a room – and froze. Sat at a piano was a young woman. She was blonde, hair in tight curls, wearing a long flowing white linen dress.

She was playing the instrument with a limited amount of skill but once in a while, a wrong note made Carol wince. Carol herself had never learned piano – no one in her family was very musically inclined – but that didn't mean she wanted to hear whatever this was she was hearing, quite so discordantly.

A well-dressed, bearded man stood up from a huge winged armchair, its back to the pianist, which is why Carol hadn't spotted him.

"Grace, my dear, you simply have to concentrate."

"I'm sorry, Papa," Grace replied, "but this is such a frightfully difficult piece to play."

The father was firm, but not unkind. There was a warmth in his voice. "No, it really isn't. It just takes time and concentration. It's London Season soon and you need to debut there, and good young men will want young ladies who can read, sew and play piano."

Carol wasn't sure what shocked her more, the antediluvian ideas being spouted or the sudden realisation that whilst she was right about *where* she was, because this was absolutely Anderson Lewis House, she wasn't quite positive about *when* she was. This wasn't a couple of actors practising a theatre show, this was real.

She wasn't in the 1970s any longer. No – somehow she appeared to be in the 1770s.

The 1770s.

She let that sink in.

At first it seemed absurd. But then again, she'd been to other planets, talked to a librarian who resembled a walrus, and picked fruit from a living tree who had told her their life story from Sapling to Ancient. The concept of actual time travel should seem no more absurd than that. Peter the Time Guardian had proven that a while back when they'd had an adventure together. But to actually time-travel herself...

Gosh.

Still, she had the evidence of her own eyes.

"The King is going to reveal you himself," the father was saying to Grace. "There is no greater honour that can be bestowed upon the McAllister family. Your mother would have been so proud."

King? Must be King George, so yes this had to be when the house itself was built.

"John? Stephen?" she called out with her mind.

Nothing. Somehow this didn't surprise her. "TIM?" she gave telepathy one last attempt.

"They won't hear you," said a voice that wasn't Grace's or her father's.

Carol looked around, trying to find the source of the voice. It was male but most definitely younger than Mr McAllister.

Far away, at the end of the corridor was the ghost boy who had grabbed her hands during the séance.

But that voice had been close.

"Hullo," it said again. "I'm Josh."

"Hullo, Josh," Carol replied out loud then immediately regretted it. Grace and her father would hear her.

She threw a look towards them, but neither had heard her. Or, she finally realised, seen her.

"They can't see or hear you, Carol," Josh said.

Again, she glanced back out into the corridor, where the ghost boy stood so far away.

"Yes, it's me. I can talk to you without speaking," he said. "I don't know how, though."

"It's called telepathy, Josh. Why don't you come here?"

At which point Josh suddenly was there. Right in front of her. Like he'd jaunted. But no lights, no sound created by air molecules being shifted around. Carol took an involuntary step back and the ghost boy, Josh, smiled.

"Sorry, didn't mean to scare you?"

"Who are you?"

"Told you, I'm Josh. Joshua Newman. I can think myself into places."

"I see. Hello, Joshua Newman. I'm Carol MacNeil. But you know that, don't you? You read my mind."

"I did what?"

"How did you know my name?"

"Oh. 'Read your mind'. Yes, I see. I can't read books and lists and things, but I can read minds. I like that description!" He grinned and his big blue eyes stared into her, a fierce intelligence behind them that belied his eighteenth-century appearance.

He reminded Carol a bit of Stephen when they'd first met. All cheek and cockiness, but incredibly smart.

"Did you do this, Josh?"

"Do what?"

"Bring me here. To the past."

Before Josh could reply, a voice from the room barked out. "Joshua Newman? What are you doing up here?"

Carol realised that whilst he couldn't see her, Grace's father could evidently see Josh.

Josh snatched his cap off his head and bowed slightly. "Sorry, Mister McAllister, my dad sent me up to check if any of the dust had blown back into the rooms."

"Then he should have checked himself. Sending a boy up to Miss Grace's room!"

Josh's eyes raised just enough so he could see Grace McAllister. "Sorry, Miss." He gave her a small smile that Mr McAllister couldn't see.

"Oh Father, don't be cross with little Josh. He was just doing what he was told." Grace stepped towards the doorway and pointed to the ground where Josh was standing. "But you'll need to get Florence to clean up the hallway. Look at the mud and soot you've trodden in."

"Sorry, Miss. Right away, Miss."

Josh turned and started to walk away, back down the long corridor he'd jaunted along seconds earlier.

"You can follow me," he said telepathically to Carol. "They won't see you."

Carol was looking at the muddy boot prints on the floor, remembering what Lefty had told them all about the muddy boot prints the Conner-Allens had been plagued by one night. The same ones Carol had peripherally seen with her own 'second-sight'.

Carol jaunted after Josh and caught up with him.

"I thought you were a ghost back in 1973," Carol said. "I'm very relieved to find that you're not really dead."

Josh stopped walking and looked up at her, his blue eyes glistening beneath the soot and muck on his face. And just as he had back in the Conner-Allens' room during the séance, he grabbed both her hands in his.

"Oh, don't worry, Carol. I'm dead all right. I'm a ghost."

*

John and Stephen had jaunted into the grounds of Anderson Lewis House just far enough away that anyone watching from the building wouldn't be able to see them.

Silently, but with practised ease, the two young men had then moved from tree to bush, slowly but surely getting closer to the front of the house.

Stephen nudged John and nodded with his head towards the two vehicles parked out front: a Triumph motorcycle and a silver Ford Granada. "Someone's got money," he said telepathically to John.

John nodded, but then added a terse "Don't get distracted," just to remind Stephen how urgent their mission was.

Both of them had called out for Carol the moment they had arrived but were met with silence.

"TIM, can you read Carol at all?"

"I'm sorry John, I can only hear you and Mr Jameson, and his predilection for fast cars."

Stephen grinned. TIM had never called him 'Mr Jameson' before. Made him sound very grown up. Mind you, it also made him sound like his dad, and—

"Come on," hissed John and almost dragged Stephen towards the gravel driveway.

However, they stopped very suddenly when the doors to the Granada opened. Someone who Stephen assumed to be Mr Conner-Allen got out of the driver's side, and from the front passenger seat emerged a youngster, about Stephen's own age. A younger girl got out of the back.

Without saying a word, the Conner-Allen family walked into their house via the front door.

Stephen saw John was frowning.

"That was weird—" he started to say telepathically, but John shot him such a look that Stephen shut up instantly.

John then did something Stephen had never heard him do before. He began humming. Not loudly, but out loud. The sort of way Stephen's mum often did when she was hanging out the washing or doing the ironing.

John was giving Stephen a fixed look as he hummed, and a minute nod of the head and a frown.

Stephen didn't understand at first until John's next nod was accompanied by a fractionally louder second of humming before it dropped down again.

Thinking he understood what John wanted, Stephen began humming. Thank god John didn't want him to sing – that wasn't something he'd inflict on anyone.

Neither of them were humming the same tune, but it didn't seem to matter to John and they headed towards the car.

John was immediately at the driver's side, looking in through the window. Stephen joined him and realised John was fixated on the keys in the ignition.

Stephen stopped humming to say, "Who leaves their keys in the ignition when the engine's off?"

John ceased humming too but indicated for Stephen to start again. "Even in the middle of nowhere that seems an odd thing to do," he agreed, then restarted his humming.

Both Tomorrow People finally entered Anderson Lewis Hall, still quietly humming.

A weird tableau greeted them.

Mr Conner-Allen and the two children were just standing in the hall. The lad was taking his coat off and hanging it on a peg, and the father was picking a newspaper up off the hallway table.

And then, bizarrely, the lad put his coat back on and the father replaced the paper. A moment later, the boy took off and re-hung his coat, the father picked up the paper. A moment then, the paper went down, the coat was put back on.

Stephen realised John was counting on his fingers the time between each movement. Six, seven, eight. Then the routines began again.

Oddest of all was the fact that none of them had acknowledged the strangers in their midst.

John turned on his heel and went back outside.

Stephen followed. John was back at the car, staring again at the car. He tried to open the door but it wouldn't budge.

How do you lock keys inside a car, still in the ignition? Stephen wanted to ask this, but instead carried on humming. He didn't know what his leader was up to, but so much weird was going on right now, he opted to follow his lead.

John was still staring at the car door. Then he raised an eyebrow and, still humming, smiled slightly. He threw a look back at the house then back inside the car. Stephen joined him and watched as the keys inside started turning slowly. John's face was screwed up in concentration. And then the car's engine nosily roared into life.

Stephen jumped and looked to the front door, expecting to see Mr Conner-Allen bolt out.

Nothing happened.

John telekinetically turned the engine off.

He indicated for Stephen to follow him back inside.

The three Conner-Allens were still stood there, going through their repeated every eight-seconds ritual.

Humming louder (so Stephen did the same) John wandered further into the house. He indicated for Stephen to go upstairs, while he implied he was going to go left. Before they separated, John gave him the 'keep humming' look again. Stephen didn't understand why but gave John a thumbs up and ascended to the first floor of the house.

He looked into a couple of empty bedrooms and then opened the door to what seemed to be a playroom for the kids. Standing at the centre, vacuum cleaner in hand, was who he guessed was Mrs Conner-Allen.

She was pushing the vacuum across the carpet. It wasn't switched on but she didn't seem aware of this. She pushed it back and forth across the carpet, then round a table and then…

And then she started repeating the pattern. As Stephen watched, she moved the vacuum over the same bit of carpet, round the same table. Then started again. Stephen counted like John had. Sixteen seconds her routine took.

He was about to report this back to John when his own humming made him opt not to. Whatever reason John had for wanting them to hum, it meant they couldn't hum and telepathically talk at the same time.

Better to report this in person, so Stephen headed back downstairs.

He found John down a corridor, outside a door to a room, his hand hovering near the handle, a levered type on a metal plate.

However, it wasn't moving, like the car keys had.

John saw Stephen and pointed towards the room, then gave a thumbs up.

Stephen understood – they needed to get inside.

He pointed to his jaunting belt, but John shook his head and draw his finger across his throat.

Jaunting was dangerous? Since when, Stephen wondered.

John indicated he should join him, pointing at the handle. Stephen shrugged. Kenny was the expert at moving objects like that. And John had clearly been practising. But Stephen had not really focussed on doing that, despite TIM's frequent instance that he ought to train. Stephen now wished he'd listened.

John stopped humming and sighed.

Stephen stopped humming too, but said nothing, out loud or telepathically.

John smiled at him. Stephen guessed he'd done something right then.

At which point John did something extraordinary, and out of character for him. He raised his leg and gave the door such a savage kick, it was guaranteed to splinter the wood and wrench it open.

Instead, John was pushed away from the door and into the wall.

He got up, blowing air out of his lungs. And finally spoke. "Newton proven. Someone or something doesn't want us to get into this room. What do you think, TIM?"

This was the first contact they had made with the Lab in nearly ten minutes. "John, I think you should come back to the Lab," said TIM. "Carol obviously isn't there. We can regroup and formulate a new plan."

Stephen frowned. That was a bit defeatist, especially for TIM.

He was about to say something but another of John's armoury of looks stopped him. "Good idea, TIM. We'll be back in a minute."

Then John pointed at his jaunting belt and with another look, this one apparently saying 'This could go disastrously wrong'. He pointed at himself, at Stephen and then at the door.

Stephen wasn't sure this would work – after all whatever was keeping them out threw John's kinetic energy back at him seconds ago. "We're coming back to the Lab now," John announced but shook his head at Stephen and again indicated the room.

Stephen again nodded his understanding.

"On a count of three, TIM. One. Two. Three."

Stephen jaunted at the same time as John, but not back to the Lab.

Both of them materialised inside the room.

And Stephen roared in pain.

*

Three Days Earlier…

Tom and Jack had finished their shift and were now sat in the Dog and Whistle, generally reckoned to be the best hostelry Woffley Hoo had to offer. Bearing in mid it was the *only* pub Woffley Hoo had to offer, competition wasn't exactly queueing up to take away that 'generally reckoned' title.

Truth was, it was a perfectly adequate pub in a perfectly adequate village not far from the perfectly adequate general hospital in Hitchin where Tom and Jack spent most of their days ferrying the injured, aged and occasionally bewildered towards in their ambulance.

"Evenin', Tom," said Sophia the barmaid. "Usual?"

"Please. Better make Jack's a big one though. He's a bit shaken up."

"Oh no – what happened, Jack?"

Whatever Jack replied, Sophia couldn't understand it. His Dunfermline accent got too broad by the end of a long shift, and no one in Hertfordshire had much chance of making out more than every third word. Tom, over the years, had become an expert at translating, but Jack was so worked up tonight, even he was having difficulty.

"I drove today," Tom explained, "so Jack sat in the back with the patients. Last one today was a real nasty one. Poor old dear was attacked in her home."

Sophia winced. "Oh it's a rotten world we live in, Tom, I say it's a rotten world."

Tom nodded. "Didn't seem to have taken nothing, mind. Just made a mess of the place and the old dear. Doctors reckon she'll recover in time, and her family are with her now."

Jack shouted something incomprehensible in his Fife brogue, as Tom passed him his glass.

"Yeah, mate, I hear ya." Tom nipped back to the bar to retrieve his pint of beer. "It's really horrible. Apparently, all she said to Jack in the back of the ambulance was that she'd been attacked by her own ghost. Really shook poor Jack up."

The barmaid nodded. "I can imagine, Tom. I say I can imagine." Then she frowned. "Did she mean she thought her house was haunted?"

Jack grumbled something again.

Tom nodded. "Jack reckons she believes that a ghost actually attacked her." He lowered his voice. "I think Jack believes in spirits, and I don't mean the ones you're serving him by the dram. So I think this old biddy going on about a ghost has made him nervous about going home tonight." Tom pointed at the bottle of Johnnie Walker Sophia had in her hand. "I reckon he'll have emptied that before I drop him off tonight. Good job we've got a day off tomorrow.'

Sophia patted Tom's arm. "Hope you're okay too, mate."

Tom nodded. "I'm fine. It's the family I feel sorry for. Half of them all turned up on motor bikes at the hospital. I don't think they're prepared for just how confused and beat up she is." He threw back most of his pint in one go. "Give us a half, and that'll be me on pop for the rest of the night. Can't afford to lose my licence over this."

As Tom took the bottle of whisky over to Jack, Sophia got out her notebook and added the toll so far tonight to Tom's tab.

*

And Back Again To The Present…

For most 14-year-old boys, most of their entry into adulthood is based around rock n roll, getting a taste of alcohol or cigarettes without their parents finding out, playing football, getting a taste of weed, also without their parents finding out, and most importantly, discovering girls.

Talking telepathically, learning to move objects with their minds, teleporting instantaneously, and watching the sunrise on Rexil 4 are not generally considered rites of passage for most boys in their early teens.

And whilst Stephen was relatively happy to sacrifice most of the former for the latter and enjoy his life as one of the Tomorrow People, it did bring with it something else most other 14-year-old boys didn't experience: being attacked, stunned, knocked out, tied up, threatened with death, and the one Stephen remembered with more clarity than anything else: utter, primal, terrifying unending pain. Pain that seemed to feature everything inside his head being raked across by a million tiny, poisoned fingernails. When that pain occurred, knocking out, stunning and death were all desirable to him if it would make that specific searing pain stop.

The one time he had really experienced that level of pain had been a few months before when he and Carol had unexpectedly come across a creature known as a Medusa whilst floating in space. Not only did it disable and cancel out their special powers, it felt as if it did it in the way described above but multiplied by one hundred.

After the Medusa was dealt with, a shaken Stephen rationalised that he was probably/possibly/hopefully (delete as applicable) never likely to encounter anything that hurt him as much as that did ever again.

Until he jaunted into the locked room in Anderson Lewis House, with John, he had no idea just how wrong he had been.

The saving grace, if there were one, was that unlike with the Medusa, this pain (imagine the above but now magnified by five hundred) only lasted about five seconds.

Stephen wasn't one to cry easily, his father – a doctor – had always said boys crying was a sign of weakness. Right now, he lay on the floor, curled up foetally, sobbing his heart out at just how much pain he had just encountered, and he didn't care who knew.

Luckily for Stephen, the only person who did know was John. And as Stephen's head swum back into clarity and consciousness, he was mildly relieved to see that John's tear-stained face matched his own.

"What the hell was that?" he managed to rasp.

John wiped his face on his sleeve. "I don't know. And I'm not sure I want to find out. But at least it stopped quickly enough."

Stephen's first instinct was to ask TIM for help, but then he remembered John's strange behaviour and general unwillingness to talk to TIM over the past twenty minutes or so.

He was therefore surprised when John called out to TIM himself. He was even more surprised to realise that all he heard was John shouting TIM's name. It didn't echo in his head; it was purely verbal.

Stephen tried to use telepathy himself, not towards TIM but to Carol. To see if whatever they had just gone through had brought them any closer to finding her.

But he couldn't.

He looked across the room, saw a chair and imagined himself sitting on it. That should have been a split-second jaunt.

Nothing happened.

"Medusa," he muttered.

"Sorry?" said John.

"It's like the Medusa all over again. My powers, they're gone."

"Nullified," John corrected him. "Our powers can't go, only be blocked, hopefully temporarily. But yes, you're right. Right now, we are just saps."

Stephen hauled himself up. "Okay, mind telling me what all that humming was about?"

John smiled grimly. "Have you ever noticed that whenever we talk to TIM, he always uses our first names. Almost every sentence he speaks will include 'Stephen' or 'John' or 'Kenny' or 'Carol'. He doesn't do it when talking to the saps like Ginge or Chris or Lefty, but to a Tomorrow Person, he does."

"And?"

"It's a safety protocol. It's a split second where his biometrics kick in and he ensures that he's really talking to us, that we're who we say we are."

"That's clever. Weird, but clever."

John nodded. "it's a protocol I set up when he was first built and one he agreed to. As a result, if ever he is in trouble and, more importantly, he feels he or the Lab have been compromised, I told him to use a surname not a first name. His way of telling us there's something wrong."

"Of course," Stephen said. "He called me Mr Jameson." He shrugged. "And I just thought it was out of respect."

"So," John continued, "the humming was to telepathically block anyone else listening in. From now on until we know what's going on, not only can't we rely on TIM, we can't be sure we're even talking *to* the real TIM."

"Right now we couldn't talk to him even if we wanted to."

"No, this whole room is locked in a null field, designed to keep us out. We only got in because we did something totally unexpected and deliberately walked into its trap."

"Yes, and a world of pain, thanks very much." Then Stephen frowned at John. "Wait a minute, you mean this null field of yours is alive?"

"Sentient certainly. And probably focussed through the old lady sat in the dark over there."

Stephen followed John's eyeline and realised for the first time that they were sharing the room with what he could only assume was Lefty's Aunt June, aka Madam Juniper Rose.

Certainly she looked every inch the eccentric medium. "What do you think happened?"

John shrugged. "Maybe she was a better medium than we thought, and she actually summoned something."

"A ghost?"

"Rationally that seems unlikely. But certainly something powerful. Powerful enough to freeze her, and project a null field throughout this house. Temporal elastic that's decreasing as it goes further."

"Why'd you say that?"

"Because she's frozen. The dad and kids out there are able to go through the motions for eight seconds, but outside the house, they were able to move freely."

"I forgot." Stephen could have kicked himself. "The mum's upstairs. Takes sixteen seconds for her elastic to stretch."

John nodded, "But deliberately contained within the house."

Stephen frowned. "Okay, so it's nullified our special powers but if it's frozen her, and slowed the others down at differing points, how come you and I can walk and talk in here so easily?"

"Eye of the storm perhaps? Or maybe some vestige of our powers allows our function?"

"Oh boys, you are missing the obvious."

Both of them turned to face Juniper Rose, who was clearly no longer frozen.

"And that is?" asked John, clearly trying not to suggest he was thrown in any way by her sudden animation.

"It's a trap. I have you two. I have TIM. And I so nearly had Carol, but I will."

"You're not Lefty's Auntie at all," Stephen said.

Juniper Rose clapped slowly, and demonstrably sarcastically. "Alas Auntie June had a little mishap a few days back and is currently under the very good care of the local NHS. Now shall we have a nice cream tea and discuss how you are going to help me destroy this planet?"

"I don't think so," John said.

"Oh, TIM?" said Juniper Rose.

"John," Stephen cried. "It was her voice we heard in the Lab. The psychic storm. It was her!"

"Of course it was. Silly boys, so slow on the uptake. You're supposed to be the future saviours of this planet, but you couldn't figure out that your 'sentient nullfield' was sitting in the room with you. Bless your silly little heads. Now where were we? Oh yes. TIM?"

"Yes, Juniper Rose?"

"TIM!" John shouted. "Override her."

"I'm sorry, John, I can't do that." TIM sounded most despondent.

"Now boys, don't fight over my computer. TIM, cream tea for three please."

With a shimmer, a cake rack with scones, jam and cream appeared, alongside a huge silver repoussé teapot, a jug of milk, plus three fine bone-china cups and saucers.

"Shall I be mother?" asked Juniper Rose, as she began pouring. "No sugar, TIM? Good, terribly bad for the teeth." She waved to the seats beside her at the table. "Do sit down."

"No, thank you," John said.

"Sit! Down!" Juniper Rose's voice was instantly harsh, commanding and vicious, as if it had been summoned from the depths of hell itself. It was the same tone she had used in the Lab.

John and Stephen found themselves walking to the same seats that, unknown to them, the Conner-Allens had occupied earlier that afternoon.

Stephen did everything he could to avoid actually walking to the seat, but his legs ignored him – it was like being a puppet. He sat, as did John.

As Juniper Rose passed the tea around, Stephen found himself lifting his cup and sipping the tea.

"Scone? No, perhaps not. Have to watch our waistlines don't we. After all, those jaunting belts of TIM's are already a bit snug."

"Who are you?" Stephen asked.

"Better question, "John interrupted. "*What* are you?"

Juniper Rose sipped her own tea. "I know it's the height of bad manners," she said, "but I'll answer a question with another question. You folk call yourself the Tomorrow People. *Homo superior*. More accurately *homo novus*. You are the first of your kind, right?"

John nodded. "I was first. The others followed. Soon more and more will break out and join us. And probably fight you."

Juniper Rose reached out and stroked his cheek. "Dear sweet naïve thing that you are, young Mr Dixon. Oh, and dear sweet naïve and *wrong* thing. You aren't the first. You about the thousandth, maybe even five thousandth. I lost count, you see. But rest assured, I was the first."

Stephen gasped. Juniper Rose patted the back of his hand. It felt cold to him. Cold and dead.

"You see, dear sweet ones, I too am a Tomorrow Person. The very first and, I have decided, the very last too."

*

Carol found herself standing in a beautiful room, huge silk curtains hanging from the ceiling, surrounding a massive four poster bed.

On it sat someone that Carol recognised from paintings she had seen at the National Gallery. The white face, the flame red hair, the high collared dress. Courtiers fussed around her as she got dressed for a dinner engagement, going by the words being spoken.

"Milady," one of the ladies-in-waiting bobbed. "The Duke of Alencon has arrived."

"And?"

"And Sir William is most concerned that you should be ready to greet him at your earliest convenience."

"I know, I know." Queen Elizabeth sighed. "Is my Lord Dudley here yet?"

"Many hours hence, milady."

The Queen smiled. "Fetch a pageboy. I would have him take a missive to Robert, warning him to stay away from the dinner this evening. One would not wish to see Sir William in shock if both Robert Dudley and Francis of Alencon met face to face." Then the Queen laughed. "Actually, I should enjoy that greatly, but I fear the three menfolk would not see the funny side."

The ladies-in-waiting all giggled appreciatively and as Carol watched, a door opened and a young, well-dressed pageboy entered, and the Queen passed him a letter.

"Joshua Newman, take this to Lord Robert Dudley forthwith. No stopping for anything."

The pageboy bowed, said "Your Majesty", took the letter and as he turned, Carol saw the face. Clean, neat and tidy, nice clothes. But those blue eyes gave it away instantly.

"Josh!" she said aloud, knowing no one could hear her.

"Carol," he replied in her head. "Follow me."

She did as she was told and as they entered the hallway outside the Queen's chamber, he once again took both her hands in his.

*

Images flashed through Carol's head. She saw Josh in so many different guises, but always about thirteen years old. He was the servant to a Roman Senator. The son of an Egyptian pharaoh. The cabin boy on a Spanish trading ship. The farmer's son during a Viking raid. A trader's boy in Babylon. So many different guises, different races, different countries, but everywhere he took her through time, he was always, well, *him*. Always thirteen years old. Those blue eyes always staring at her at the last moment, promising another random ride through time. Josh. Yeshua. Joshua. Juosue. Giosue. Iokua. Iesous. Gishu. Yueshuya… so many identities. But one thing was the same, no matter how out of place it must have seemed to those around him. No matter how many derivations of Josh he lived through, he was always Newman. No translations. Not iterations. Always his last name was Newman.

Carol's reverie was broken finally when she was standing outside a cave. The air was cloying, and she coughed slightly. It was hot. Not scorchingly so, but enough to make Carol wish she'd had time to pack beach clothing. Stifling heat, humid. Sticky.

She looked around the empty plains that surrounded her. No one. No buildings. No markers or guides to tell her what place and time Josh Newman had brought her to now.

A cry stabbed through her brain, raw telepathy of a kind Carol hadn't felt since she herself first broke out. Images flashed through her mind. A playing field. Girls playing rounders during school holidays. Her sense of falling, voices in her head, pounding, shouting, throbbing as her mind opened up to the new world of the Tomorrow People and through it all, the calm voices of John. Of TIM.

But their voices weren't here now. There were no voices to speak of, just screeching and shouting and yelling. Incoherent loud voices, making sound and fury but with no words. And then:

"Carol!"

It was the only thing she could make out.

"Carol!"

It was Josh, she knew that, but he sounded desperate, pained.

Instinctively, Carol walked inside the cave, and was immediately cooled by the rocks. She marched further in until a sight she could never have imagined stopped her in her tracks.

A group of tiny people, pygmies really, she guessed, were scurrying around, rudely shoving one another aside.

Dark skinned, naked, eyes wide in fear.

Of course, she was invisible to them, so she got closer, wanting to see what was causing the fuss.

"Carol!"

And then she understood. Lying on a rough bed of bush grass, was a child. And whereas everyone around her had big brown eyes, she recognised Josh's blue eyes in this distorted… yes that was the word, *Neanderthal* body.

"Goodness," she said to herself. "*Homo sapiens*. The dawn of man. I'm right back at the beginnings of modern life."

Josh was thrashing about, like he was possessed.

"Carol!" was in her head louder, but Carol still couldn't use her powers to reply.

Josh was breaking out. Of course, he was a Tomorrow Person.

Which meant, back in Grace McAllister's room in the 1770s, when he pretended not to understand the 'read your mind' stuff, he'd been, well, lying. Testing her perhaps. Because he must have known everything all along.

Gosh, he must have been the first, and amongst his powers, perhaps a Methuselah-like ability to live forever, trapped in the body of a thirteen-year-old.

It had never occurred to Carol that there might have been Tomorrow People before her and John and Kenny and Stephen. But of course, she remembered what Juniper Rose had said. Second-Sight. Witchcraft. All interpretations of the Tomorrow People's powers across the ages. So there must have been Tomorrow People throughout history, but lost, alone, unable to gather and become a unified group as she and her friends had managed.

Now here he was. The start of the evolution towards *homo superior*. Literally, a New Man. Joshua *Newman*.

Her train of thought was interrupted as a new figure walked through the crowd. The Neanderthal pygmies all dropped to the floor in reverence and Carol assumed this was the tribe's version of Queen Elizabeth the First, or Caesar, or any of the myriad other powerful leaders she had witnessed courtesy of Josh's teleportation.

The figure knelt beside the thrashing boy and took his hand. Instantly he stopped jerking spasmodically and instead started to breathe easily, to relax.

The figure put a hand to early Josh's temple.

And Carol heard a voice echo in her head. Not Josh this time. This voice was soft, feminine, nurturing.

"Do not fear, boy. You are *not* the first, but you *are* the second. You will survive, you will grow strong because you have the power within you. The pain you feel in your head, the noises, the rage, will

78

go away if you focus. Focus on my voice. Listen and picture what I say. I want you to imagine that your mind is a fist. A great big fist. Clenched tight. Now, let it open, slowly. Don't let any other thoughts come into your head. Just think of the fist opening very slowly, like a flower."

Carol gasped out loud. Those words. The words John had used on her. Used on Kenny. Words she herself had used on Stephen. The Tomorrow People litany.

But in truth they were words spoken by the first Tomorrow Person to the second, aeons before Carol and any of her friends were born!

Also, at a time when language did not even exist. That's how advanced these Tomorrow People were compared to their pygmy peers.

"That's amazing," she said aloud.

And the primeval person tending Josh slowly turned and looked in her direction. They had heard her speak.

"Not possible," said a voice in her head that she somehow knew was this earliest Tomorrow Person.

Leaving Josh's side, the tiny person hobbled over quickly, ignoring the confusion from all the other pygmy people, who couldn't see Carol.

The little person glared up at her.

And Carol realised she was staring at the face of Juniper Rose as she must have looked one-hundred and twenty-five thousand years ago.

Juniper Rose screeched one sentence inside Carol's head before everything went blank.

"Get out of here!"

Episode Three

The sudden arrival of Carol's form in the little room took Stephen and John by surprise.

To be frank, it seemed to take Juniper Rose aback slightly too, but she recovered her composure quickly enough breathing out a "oh how interesting" while pouring the tea.

John and Stephen tried to get out of their seats and go to Carol, but they couldn't.

Juniper Rose smiled at them.

"Naughty boys, did I give you permission to leave the table?"

Carol wasn't moving. Although Stephen didn't know it, she was actually in exactly the same position she had been in when the Conner-Allens saw her seemingly swallowed by shadows earlier.

"What have you done to her?" he snapped at Juniper Rose.

She just shrugged and passed over the milk jug. He ignored it.

"Miss MacNeil's current problems are nothing to do with me. I was astonished as she was when it all went a little tipsy-wipsy earlier, before I was able to sort things out, get rid of those annoying… saps I believe is the term you use, and try and find Carol." She held her hands out, as if that explained everything.

"That explains nothing," John said.

Stephen nodded, keeping an eye on the frozen-in-place Carol.

"This whole planet is a mass of useless saps, a dead-end genetic slurry that this planet needs to be rid of," Juniper Rose said. "The same way you'd rid a pussy cat of a parasitic tapeworm. Or fleas. Mankind has outlived any usefulness it might have had the potential for. It has betrayed this world and squandered the opportunities it offered. Only *homo novus* offers the true path to glory for the world. You Tomorrow People see yourselves as gardeners, helping mankind flourish, nurturing and cultivating their best traits, protecting them against themselves, growing a future for them. As the very first of your kind, who 'broke out' as you call it aeons ago and immediately saw my own potential, I have to say you are very disappointing. So, here's my offer: help me eradicate the parasites and fleas and we can populate this world with nothing but Tomorrow People. The superior evolutionary next step. Those who truly deserve to dominate."

John shrugged. "And if we don't?"

Madam Juniper Rose, or whatever she really was, smiled at him. "Then you are no better than those fleas and will be erased along with them. I can always wait till better Tomorrow People come along, Tomorrow People with the foresight to recognise their superiority and use it to aid me. Tomorrow People unburdened by your mediocre genetic morality. It might take ten years, or twenty. Or thirty. But I can wait. It only takes one mutant Tomorrow Person with the ability to kill, and the world is mine."

"You are mad," Stephen said.

"Dangerous thing to say to the woman who holds your life in her hands. Or mind, if you want accuracy."

Stephen didn't care. "History is full of people like you. We learn about them at school. Dictators and dominators and they always lose in the end, because the saps we protect are better than you think. They are worth fighting for."

There was silence. Then: "Oh sorry, were you waiting for a round of applause for that little speech, young man? Bad luck."

Stephen just stared at her. "So if you really were born back in the time of the dinosaurs, or whenever, you must be very lonely. Is that why you are such a—"

"Stephen," John said warningly.

"Well…" the younger lad muttered.

"But Stephen has a point," John continued. "Don't you see? The difference between us is we have families. Families and friends who aren't Tomorrow People. They are the ones we fight for. If you are alone, that's why you can't see why they must be protected."

"Oh, she *has* family," said a new voice.

Stephen felt his heart rate increase momentarily. A young boy was floating, half-transparent in the air above the table.

Like a ghost.

"I'm her son."

The ghost floated down until he bisected the table, intangibly walking through it towards Carol. He grabbed her hands and with a cry, Carol woke up. And smiled. "Hullo, Joshua!"

Then Carol realised where she was and who was in the room with her.

"John, Stephen, that's not Lefty's Auntie June. That's—"

"Yeah, we know," Stephen said.

"I can't move," Carol said. "My legs aren't working."

"That's down to her too," John said.

Josh floated back up, hovering cross-legged just above the table. "No it's not," he said. "It's an illusion. You could move whenever you wanted to. She's just implanted a suggestion in all your heads that you can't. She's very clever, my mother."

"No, really, we can't move," John insisted.

Juniper Rose laughed. "The Tomorrow People are powerful, Joshua, but not as powerful as me."

"As us," Josh corrected her.

"Why don't you materialise properly?" Juniper Rose taunted. "Show them how powerful you are. It must be terribly exhausting doing all this ghost stuff."

Josh looked at Carol who nodded. "He can't," she said. "Because he's dead. He told me."

Juniper Rose frowned. "No, he's not, Carol. You know that, you've been zipping and zapping all through history with him. He wasn't remotely dead."

"I've been dead for one-hundred and twenty-five thousand years, Mother," Josh said. "Give or take a few decades, it's hard to keep exact track as no one invented a universally accepted calendar until the sixteenth century."

But Carol was confused. "But one thing Juniper Rose says is true. Other than here, everywhere else you were a solid real little boy. I was the ghost really."

Josh shook his ghostly head. "I've been a psychic projection, nothing more. My real body, the real me, died in that cave, when you distracted my mother. But I have a special power that none of your modern Tomorrow People have. The power of bilocation. I can project myself into two places at once. I shared that with you Carol, too. On our journey through time, whilst your actual body was sat in this room the whole time. But masked from anyone being able to see it."

Carol was horrified. "You mean… I killed you?"

Josh shook his head. "Not at all. I was already dying, but you distracting her gave me the boost I needed to let go of my physical body and move beyond. To bilocate."

"TIM, are you getting all this?" John telepathically said.

"Yes John, I am. And it's fascinating. But it does us little good whilst I am under Juniper Rose's power of suggestive immobility, just as you are."

"It's rude not to talk out loud," Juniper Rose said.

John was regarding Josh, carefully. As if he trusted him only marginally more than Juniper Rose. Which, Stephen reckoned, was probably wise.

"I assume it was you that created all those poltergeist things at this house?"

Josh smiled. "Course."

"Why?"

"Two reasons. Firstly, to attract my mother there. She's been trying to track me down for centuries, posing as mediums, spiritualists, shamen, kahuna, peai, mambo…"

Juniper Rose sighed loudly.

Josh grinned at Carol, who smiled back. "I made a decision that as the world of the late twentieth century is clearly going to produce the most organised, sophisticated Tomorrow People, plus the attention of the alien worlds is upon them, this needed to be the end of the line for me. And her."

"I still don't get why," said Carol.

"Because I am exhausted," Josh said simply. "I am old. So very old, always running from my mother, always trying to stay one step ahead of witchfinders, exorcists, military types. I decided that it was finally time for the very first to hand over this planet's protection to the very latest." Josh waved his arm around to imply John, Carol and Stephen. "And best."

"Oh, pass me a bucket," Juniper Rose raised her eyes heavenwards and yawned.

Ignoring her, Josh leaned over towards John. "By the way, keep an eye on the military in this time period. You can never trust them and, take it from someone who has seen your kind flourish in other eras, not every Tomorrow Person has the ethics you do, John."

Juniper Rose suddenly slammed her fists down on the table. "Do belt up, Joshua. You are getting very dull and boorish in your old age."

Stephen's leg spasmed slightly. Like cramp. Was she letting her guard down?

Carol brought her attention to Josh again. "But you are still only thirteen years old. What happens to you if you stay here?"

Josh stared at his mother. "That depends on her. We are linked – and despite appearances, don't forget we are many hundreds of thousands of years old. If she wants to live and I want to die, we have an impasse. If she's willing to accept our time has come, we can both rest finally. All I have to do is fully materialise here and now, using my bilocation powers one last time, and it's done. I will start to age and grow old, naturally. Enjoy my next, and last, sixty years or so." He threw a smile at Juniper Rose, but there was no mirth behind his eyes. "My mother will do the same. But far less than sixty years for her I imagine."

"You will both become human? Saps?"

Juniper Rose laughed. "Goodness no. We'll still have our powers. Far stronger and better than any of you lot. But yes, for us both to exist at the same time, we lose our immortality. Which," and she addressed this directly to Josh, "is not going to happen."

Josh ignored her. "That's why I took you through time, Carol. You are the most empathic of this team, the most open to new things.' He threw a look at the boys. "No disrespect."

"None taken," Stephen lied.

"Seriously, you underestimate Carol's powers. Stephen, you are practising your healer powers.

Rudimentary now, but in a while, you'll have the power to bring back the recently dead. John, your psychokinetic talent is superb. Another few years, you could dismantle and rebuild a wristwatch without taking the back off. Your friend Kenny, his psychometry is amazing – he can read any inanimate object, tell you where it's been, who has handled it. Never mind the telepathy, teleportation and basic telekinesis you all share. All you are going to do is get better."

"And me?"

"Carol, you are a nurturer, an empath of astonishing quality. You create an aura of calm and joy in people. If you worked for the police, you would make a fantastic hostage negotiator. You may think it's a passive power, but it makes you the most powerful Tomorrow Person of this era. It's an amazing and unique ability and that's why I took you with me. I needed you back in time, to alter history."

"That's not possible, Joshua," said TIM suddenly in all their heads.

"Who invited you?" Juniper Rose snapped.

"I'm sorry, but it is, TIM," Joshua corrected him. "Only tiny events, nothing capricious. But I originally died when I broke out. By using my bilocation talents, I projected myself forward, until I found the person whose innate good energy would distract my mother at the right moment, creating a slightly altered timeline where she was forced to travel after me." Josh looked at Juniper Rose. "You think you set a trap for these wonderful people, to try and use them to find me and kill me, but actually, I used them to set a trap for *you*."

And Joshua Newman suddenly became solid, standing next to Carol. "A new man in a new time," he smiled. "And there's nothing you can do to stop me."

Juniper Rose jumped out of her seat.

As did John and Stephen, aware they could finally move again.

Joshua ran round the room and grabbed Juniper Rose, both hands in his. "Welcome to mortality, Mother."

And Juniper Rose let out a terrible cry of pain and anguish.

For a moment all Carol, John and Stephen could see were two figures caught inside some kind of time storm, blurring them, shimmering them. It gave off a massive blast of air, like the one that had thrown Stephen and John around the Lab earlier.

"John," TIM's voice suddenly snapped into their heads. "I am free of her control."

"So are we," Stephen reported, trying to keep his balance.

"Jaunt back here immediately then," TIM commanded.

"We can't," Carol cried. "We may need to help Josh."

John agreed. "Also, there are saps in this house. We need to get them out."

"If Juniper Rose's power over you has ceased, it will have over them too," TIM pointed out.

Carol was reaching out to touch the vastly powerful time storm encasing Juniper Rose and Joshua Newman, but Stephen pulled her back. "There's nothing we can do for them now."

"Carol!" John shouted over the wind, to get her attention. "Help Stephen get the Conner-Allens away from here. They know you, say that the evil spirit that attacked them is free, tell them anything, but make them go away, quickly.'

With a last pained look at the time storm surrounded her new friend, Carol left the room, followed by Stephen.

*

All four members of the Conner-Allen family were huddled in the hallway, a discarded vacuum cleaner at the top of the stairs.

They spotted Carol running towards them from the direction of the séance room.

"You vanished!"

"It's gone wrong," Stephen yelled. "The demons are free. They'll kill us all."

Instead of running away, Benjamin just stared at Stephen. "And who the hell are you?"

"A good spirit, summoned here by Madam Juniper Rose," Carol lied, rather too easily for her liking. "Get your family away from here, Mr Conner-Allen. Now!"

Rather helpfully at that point, the door to the séance room at the bottom of the corridor was blown off its hinges and into the opposite wall, and threads of the time storm burst out, along with the huge wind.

Pictures, tables, rugs, everything down the corridor was swept up into the air.

"Go!" Stephen yelled.

The Conner-Allens needed no additional persuasion.

"I can't find the car keys," Benjamin yelled.

"They're in the ignition where you left them," Stephen shouted as a small chair whipped past them.

The family fled and Stephen slammed the front door shut behind them.

A second later, they heard glass shattering. "Oh right," Stephen said. "The car door was locked." Shortly after, the Ford Granada's wheels screeched on the gravel and the Conner-Allens were gone.

"They'll be back," Carol said. "Probably with the police."

"Then we better shut those two down beforehand," Stephen said, and the two Tomorrow People began the difficult journey of negotiating the wind and getting back down the corridor into the séance room.

*

John was on the floor, one hand trying to reach into the mad vortex of time and wind that surrounded Juniper Rose and Joshua Newman.

"John, no!" cried Carol, and she and Stephen fought their way in.

"We have to stop this," John gasped. "They'll bring the house down."

"Then let's do what TIM suggested, jaunt away and leave them to it," Stephen suggested. Carol and John stared at him. "All right," he said, "it was only a suggestion."

"What can we do?" Carol asked desperately.

John sighed. "Juniper Rose was frightened by us, wanting to trap us so that she could disable us all. And TIM. Which means that she sees us as a threat. Together, we could stop her."

"How?"

"I don't know. But we have powers, that's the whole reason we are Tomorrow People. We are here to save this planet and its people."

"But," Carol said, staring at what she thought might have been Josh inside the time storm, "they're our people too. The original Tomorrow People. Just like witches and soothsayers and people with second-sight all through the years. I went to their home, the original home of the first Tomorrow People. For all I know, it might have been the spot our Lab is now built on."

"No," Stephen said suddenly, "but what if this house is? Maybe that's why everything is focussed here. Josh able to project himself, Juniper Rose investigating. This place could have been the focus of paranormal activity for centuries. Millennia."

"Yes," Carol agreed. "Juniper Rose said that old Oliver McAllister was known to talk to spirits in the house. Gosh, it was probably Josh's ghost-form."

"If this *is* the first site, the birthplace of the Tomorrow People, maybe we can tap into that, use it." John was all business again. "TIM, we need to link, see into each others' minds, beyond telepathy. We need to become one."

"Yes, John," TIM replied. "I think that is wise. But dangerous."

"I can't do that," Stephen said. "I haven't trained for that yet."

"Then consider this your training, Stephen," TIM said. "I will boost you as much as I can from here."

Carol held out her hands and John and Stephen did the same, till they were all touching fingertips like they did back at the Link Table in the Lab.

"Maybe this is the origin of holding hands at a séance," Carol said.

"Concentrate," John snapped. "All of us. Concentrate on finding enough psychic power to shut this down."

Stephen felt lost for a moment. Then he remembered the litany Carol had taught him when he first broke out.

A fist. A fist opening. A flower. A foetus representing birth. Stars. Galaxies. Shadows and shapes. Seeds. Earth. Fire. Water. Air. The fist opening and closing.

He gasped. There was such a comfortable familiarity now to telepathy with John, Carol and TIM. But this... this was an intimacy that went beyond anything he'd experienced before.

He realised he was seeing powerful images in his head, memories that weren't his.

Liquids, biometrics. TIM being created, being born.

An eight-year-old John being adopted into a welcoming family, but a fire, his adopted brother dying, the grief, the pain... the guilt that the boy couldn't save... Timothy... remembering another brother, a biological brother he had been forced to leave at the orphanage... Colin... so much guilt...

Carol... moving from home to home... TV studios... A newspaper office... the girl forever being abandoned by her media-obsessed parents, passed from babysitter to babysitter... but no resentment, no anguish at this lack of love... instead, it made her bond to strangers, to those in need so much earlier than most children would...

What secrets were Carol and John seeing from him? Did he even have secrets? Was that his truth – that inside he was just dull, just average... Did he deserve to be a Tomorrow Person? Was he a failure? He would never match up to John, or any of those random lonely Tomorrow People through the ages who had somehow survived their own breaking out, which of course weak Stephen wouldn't have without Carol and John and Kenny and TIM he was so feeble, so useless, so...

With a massive yank of gravity, like being shot backwards on a roller-coaster, Stephen found himself back in the séance room.

He was still touching John and Carol's fingertips.

There was no time storm, no vortex, just a massively damaged room.

And at the heart of it, two figures, gasping for breath.

"Mortal," Joshua Newman breathed. "At last I can live. And die."

"You ungrateful, foolish child, what have you done to us?" Juniper Rose staggered as she tried to get up. "What have you done to *me*?"

"Given you freedom, Mother. We all have. All the Tomorrow People. Not just these three here but the time storm linked me with every Tomorrow Person there has ever been. Maybe some who are yet to be. I was bilocated, standing next to each of them, linked into their minds thanks to John, Stephen, Carol and TIM. A gestalt of Tomorrow People."

"I curse you, Joshua. I curse you all."

Then Juniper Rose was gone. Jaunted.

Joshua staggered and Carol broke the circle to hold him up.

"Thank you all." Josh looked up at the ceiling. "Thank you too, TIM, wherever you are."

"A pleasure, Joshua," TIM's voice echoed in all their heads. "I cannot trace where your mother has gone, I regret to say."

In the distance, they could hear police sirens.

"We ought to get out of here. Back to TIM."

"We have to take Josh with us," Carol said.

"Of course," John agreed.

"I haven't learned to jaunt long spatial distances," Josh said with a smile.

There was a warble of sound, a swirl of light and a jaunting belt materialised on the floor. Carol helped Josh put it on.

"I will give you all the help you need, Josh," TIM said in their heads.

Moments later, the police and fire service roared up to the entrance of Anderson Lewis House, parking next to an abandoned old Triumph motorbike.

Yet when they went inside, there was no sign of anyone who had the wrought the devastation they witnessed.

Not even a ghost…

*

Three days later, the Tomorrow People and their friends were in the local park, enjoying a late summer picnic that TIM had conjured up as only TIM could.

"How's your Auntie June, Lefty? Is she home now?" asked Carol.

Lefty nodded. "Yeah. Thanks."

Stephen immediately knew everything was okay again. Lefty was back to speaking in monosyllables, Ginge and his younger brother Chris were throwing a rugger ball around the park and John was sat in the shade, doing everything he could to avoid getting any kind of tan.

Carol passed a can of pop to him, so Stephen thanked her and tugged the ring pull off.

"And how are you feeling?" he said quietly to her.

Carol smiled at him. "Thank you for asking." She seemed to be thinking about her reply. "I'm all right," she finally said. "But very tired. I think being, quite literally, in two places at once is very exhausting."

Stephen nodded. "I can imagine." He shook his head. "No, I can't, actually. It's been a weird year or so since I met you lot."

"You've grown up a lot, you know," Carol said.

"Gee, thanks."

"No, seriously, you have. Being a Tomorrow Person suits you. You like all the adventures and the excitement. It seems to make you come alive."

"Well, it's given me… a purpose, I think my father would say." Stephen's eyes widened. "I don't like this; I keep saying things he'd say. Can I go back to being a kid again?"

Carol shook her head. "As Tomorrow People, I think we age mentally faster than most. I was thirteen when I broke out and I've been hanging around with John and TIM for a few years now, finding Kenny, then you. And now Joshua Newman. Look at John, he's nineteen going on ninety."

"He does like to think he's everyone's dad, doesn't he."

Carol nodded. "And I seem to be everyone's mum."

Stephen nudged her playfully. "Oh, I wouldn't say that. More the big sister I never had. More importantly, that Josh never had."

Carol shrugged. "Not what I expected." She paused, then took Stephen's hand in hers. "You have to stop thinking of yourself as a weakness, as any kind of burden or failure."

"So you did sense all that," Stephen said slightly bitterly.

Carol smiled. "Only glimpses. More… an impression. As I'm sure you got impressions and flashes of mine and John's innermost thoughts and, insecurities. Oh Stephen, I wish you could see in yourself what John and I see in you. You are going to be a teacher one day."

"No thanks, I can't wait to leave school, no plans to work there."

Carol laughed. "No, I mean a teacher of Tomorrow People. Taking all you learned from John and I, and for every new Tomorrow Person that comes along, you'll be the one who can relate best to them, make them learn how to use their powers."

"Doesn't sound like me," Stephen said. "But I'll take your word for it."

Carol looked as if she was going to add something, but then seemed to change her mind.

"You okay?"

She sighed. "I'm going to visit Josh on the Trig next week, see if he wants to settle here in the 20th century for good."

"Okay."

"Stephen, I'm thinking of staying there. For a while at least. My parents seem fine with the idea and I need a change, I need less…"

"Danger?"

"Excitement."

Stephen nodded. "I see," he said quietly. "Have you told John?"

"Not yet. But I think I should."

"When?" Stephen was full of conflicting emotions suddenly. He understood, he thought anyway, why Carol wanted the change, but he knew he'd miss her terribly. That made him feel selfish. "You were the first Tomorrow Person I ever met," he said out loud.

Carol squeezed his hand. "No time like the present," she said and got up. Stephen watched as she walked towards John, who looked up at her with a smile.

Despite all their telepathy, their powers at large, John had no idea what Carol was about to tell him.

Was this the end? Would John decide that they should all give up and go their separate ways?

"Hey," said a voice behind him. Stephen turned and couldn't help the big grin that crossed his face.

"Kenny! When'd you get back?"

"Just now. TIM said I'd find you lot out here in the park."

"Hey kid, catch," came a shout from Ginge and with expertise that Stephen was jealous of, Kenny caught the rugby ball, turned three hundred and sixty degrees with its momentum and then punted it straight back to the Harding brothers.

"Welcome home!" Ginge called, and Kenny gave him a thumbs up, before sitting back beside Stephen again.

From a few feet away, perhaps sensing this was the right thing to do, Lefty gave Kenny a nod and wandered over to join Ginge and Chris's game.

"Did you have fun being Mr Ambassador to the stars?"

Kenny laughed. "S'alright I s'pose. Not really me, is it?"

Stephen shrugged. "I dunno. I think if we put our minds to it, we can be anything we want really."

There was a silence between the friends for a moment.

"So, everyone on the Trig's been talking about this Neanderthal Tomorrow Person you lot saved," Kenny finally said. "Apparently, he wants to grow old like the rest of us now. Seems stupid if you ask me. I wouldn't mind being immortal."

"Not sure I would," Stephen said. "I can see why he wants to be normal. Well, as normal as being one of us can be."

Kenny grinned. "Tell me about it. What's his story?"

Stephen was about to explain, when he and Kenny saw John stand up from under his shady tree and give Carol a massive hug.

"What's that about?" Kenny asked. "They finally realised they're made for each other?"

Stephen sighed. "I hope not, for John's sake."

Kenny frowned, clearly not understanding. "Not my place to tell you," Stephen said, "but I'm sure Carol will."

"Okay."

Another silence. But that was okay, Stephen reckoned, because good friends don't need to fill up every second of time with talk or action. Sometimes you can just enjoy the pauses and each others' company.

Kenny opened a can of pop. "So, how'd you meet this Joshua kid then?"

Stephen laid back on the warm grass, staring at the sky as he started to talk to Kenny, pleased to have his best friend back again. "Well," he said. "It all started because of Lefty really. Lefty and his poor old Auntie June…"

Printed in Great Britain
by Amazon